THE DANGER JOE SHOW
Back to the Bayou

by Jon Buller and Susan Schade

SCHOLASTIC INC.

New York   Toronto   London   Auckland   Sydney
Mexico City   New Delhi   Hong Kong   Buenos Aires

FINNEY COUNTY PUBLIC LIBRARY
605 E. Walnut
Garden City, KS 67846

Visit Jon Buller and Susan Schade at their website: www.bullersooz.com

The authors appreciate the right to use an excerpt from *How Do Dinosaurs Say Good Night?* by Jane Yolen, illustrated by Mark Teague.
Text copyright ©2000 by Jane Yolen, illustrations copyright ©2000 by Mark Teague.

The authors would like to thank Dan Wharton, Director of the Central Park Zoo, for occasionally lending them his brain.

If you purchased this book without a cover, you should be aware that this book is stolen property. It was reported as "unsold and destroyed" to the publisher, and neither the author nor the publisher has received any payment for this "stripped book."

No part of this publication may be reproduced in whole or in part, or stored in a retrieval system, or transmitted in any form or by any means, electronic, mechanical, photocopying, recording, or otherwise, without written permission of the publisher. For information regarding permission, write to Scholastic Inc., Attention: Permissions Department, 557 Broadway, New York, NY 10012.

ISBN 0-439-40978-0

Copyright ©2003 by Jon Buller and Susan Schade. All rights reserved. Published by Scholastic Inc. SCHOLASTIC, The Danger Joe Show and associated logos are trademarks and/or registered trademarks of Scholastic Inc.

12 11 10 9 8 7 6 5 4 3 2   3 4 5 6 7 8/0

Printed in the U.S.A.   40

First printing, March 2003

Hooray for Ellanora,
the African explora!
(Let no one call her Schnorra!)
Hooray! Hooray! Hooray!

CHAPTER ONE
BEDTIME STORY

"OK, Jane," I say to my little sister. "No more fooling around. It's bedtime!"

Giggles come from under the bed.

I say, "I know you're under there, Janie."

Jane laughs out loud.

Suni laughs because Jane is laughing. And she throws her teddy bear out of the crib.

Baby-sitting isn't easy.

Suni is staying overnight at our house — in Jane's old crib.

She is Lucy's baby. And Lucy is someone we see a lot. That's because she is the producer of my dad's TV series, *The Danger Joe Show*.

My dad is Danger Joe Denim, and his show is all about wild animals.

I'm Joe Denim, Jr.

Here's what I have to do tonight: I have to read to Jane and Suni until they fall asleep. That's not as easy as it sounds.

First, I pick up Suni's teddy and give it back to her. She sucks on its ear and lies down. Good.

Next, I tell Jane to get into bed or I'm getting Mom. (The grown-ups are right downstairs. I'm not old enough to baby-sit when they go out.)

Jane climbs out from under the bed. She doesn't look sleepy at all.

"Lie down," I order.

Jane jumps into bed. She scoots way down and pulls the covers all the way up over her head.

"Come on, Jane. Don't act silly!" I say sternly.

More giggles come from under the covers.

I sigh and open the book.

I read the first page to the lump in the bed:

How does a dinosaur
say good night
when Papa comes in
to turn off the light?

Jane's head pops out. "NOT THAT ONE!"
she shouts.

"SHHHH!" I hiss at her. "Suni is just falling asleep!"

Jane claps her hand over her mouth. Then she whispers, "Tell me a *real* story."

"What do you mean?" I say. "This *is* a real story. It's your favorite book! Mom told me it was."

"No," she says. "I mean a real, *true* story. An adventure! Like Daddy tells."

"Oh," I say. "You mean like what happens when we're filming a show?"

Jane nods and smiles at me. She sits back against her pillows and holds Darleen, her toy koala, in her lap.

I say, "Uh, OK. I guess I can do that. Um, let's see. Do you want baby elephants in Africa, or kangaroos in Australia?"

"No," says Jane. "Tell me the one about the giant alligator."

"You mean Ol' Elvis? In the bayou? But you were there! You already know all about it!"

"I know," says Jane. "It's my favorite story. It's all about 'A Girl Called Jane.' You start with, *This is a story about a girl called Jane.*"

"No way!" I announce. "I'm not saying that! It's stupid!"

Jane scrunches up her face and squeezes out a few tears. "That's the way Daddy always starts!" she blubbers. And she starts making those little gasping noises that mean she's working herself up for a good bawl.

I sigh. "OK, OK," I say. "I'll do it. But no crying, or Suni will start, too."

Janie sits back against the pillows again and gives me a sweet smile.

I start:

This is a story about a girl called Jane, and about Ol' Elvis, the World's Biggest Alligator!

Jane is riding in the car with her family. They're on their way to bayou country, to film an episode of The Danger Joe Show. . . .

CHAPTER TWO
ON THE ROAD

"LOOK AT THAT!" Dad shouts. "BALD EAGLE! WHAT A GRAND OLD BIRD!"

He watches it fly overhead. Our car swerves into the other lane.

"Keep your eyes on the road, Joe," my mother says sharply.

Dad gets back in the right lane. Then he puts on his blinker, and we turn off the highway.

"Are we there?" says Jane.

"Not yet, honey," says Mom. "Just a few more hours."

Hours?! I groan. I look back out the window.

The land around here is all flat, with wavy grasses and lots of water. You can smell salt in the air.

"Is this the bayou?" I ask.

Jane bursts out laughing. You never know what will set her off. I ignore her.

"Bayous are creeks," Dad says to me. "There are bayous in the forests, and bayous in the swamps, and bayous in the marshes, like here. I guess you could say we're in *bayou country*."

Janie looks at me across the backseat and says, "Bye, you." Then she turns away.

I think she's saying 'bayou,' because that's the way you pronounce it.

Then she turns back and says, "Hello, you! HA, HA, HA!"

That's a little kid's idea of humor.

Actually, I think it's a pretty good joke for a kid. So I laugh and say, "How's BY YOU?"

Jane gets it. She says, "Where's BY YOU?"

I say, "Who's BY YOU?"

Jane gives me a sly look. Then she points at me and says, "MEATLOAFHEAD'S BY ME! HA, HA, HA!"

I'm trying to think of a good comeback when Dad interrupts us. "Who's watching out for car number two?" he says.

Car number two is Elton and Lucy. Elton is the cameraman for Dad's show. And Lucy is the producer (like I said before). She plans the show. They are following us in another car with all of the filming equipment.

Jane and I squirm around in our seat belts and try to look out the back.

"I see them!" I shout before Jane. "They're still there."

We pass a big billboard that says, "ONE HUNDRED YARDS AHEAD — WORLD'S OLDEST MAN!"

I read it out loud. "YOW!" I say. "Can we stop, Dad? That sounds interesting! How old do you think he is?"

"STOP! STOP!" yells Jane. She always has to get in on the action.

Now there's another sign, "TURN HERE. WORLD'S OLDEST MAN!", with an arrow pointing to a driveway. Dad drives right by.

"Aw, gee, Dad," I say. "Why couldn't we stop? That would have been so cool! I could have told everyone at school about it!"

"Sorry, kids," says Dad. "We can't stop at every roadside attraction. A lot of them are just scams, anyway."

"What's a scam?" I say.

"A scam is a hoax," Mom explains. "You know, a trick or a joke. For example, you might pay to see the oldest man, and it might turn out to be just a photo of an old man, or a fake mummy or something."

"A mummy?!" I say. I hadn't thought of that! What if it was a mummy?!

"A MUMMY!" shouts Jane. "I want to see the mummy!" she says.

I don't think Jane knows what mummies are.

We pass a road sign. "WORLD'S BIGGEST CRAB," I read.

"Oh, look at that, Joe!" Mom says. "Remember when we saw the 'WORLD'S BIGGEST CRAB' in Maryland?"

"Hey," I say. "How can there be more than one 'WORLD'S BIGGEST CRAB'?"

"Remember what we said about scams?" Dad asks.

Mom says, "One could be the biggest live crab, and one could be the biggest statue of a crab, or something like that."

I don't think I like the idea of tricking people that way.

"Well," says Mom, "most people know roadside attractions are just for fun. Entertainment isn't always, um, factual. But still, it helps to remember that you can't believe everything you read."

We pass another sign. "SUBSTANDARD ROAD," I read. "What does that mean?"

Dad slams on the brakes. It's a good thing we're wearing our seat belts!

Dad says, "That's our turn!" And he starts backing up. Lucy and Elton almost crash into us.

Finally, both cars are bouncing down the SUBSTANDARD ROAD. I guess substandard means it's not as smooth as a regular road.

We drive through grass that's almost as tall as our car until we come to the water's edge.

Dad points to some twisted trees full of dead sticks. "Snowy egret nests!" he says.

Everybody piles out. Janie finds a crawfish, and Elton starts filming.

Dad talks on camera. "HI! I'M DANGER JOE, AND WE ARE IN BEAUTIFUL BAYOU COUNTRY! LOOKS QUIET, DOESN'T IT? WELL, THESE MARSHES ARE TEEMING WITH WILDLIFE — ALLIGATORS, EGRETS, AND LOTS OF OTHER WONDERFUL ANI-MALS! HERE'S A LITTLE CRAWFISH. IT LOOKS LIKE A BABY LOBSTER, BUT IT'S A FULL-GROWN RED SWAMP CRAWFISH. THE MARSH IS FULL OF THEM. ONE FEMALE CAN PRODUCE ABOUT FOUR HUNDRED BABIES IN ONE SEASON! GAD-ZOOKS!"

Dad points out an alligator in the water be-low the nests. All you can see are its nostrils and eyes sticking up out of the smooth, dark water, between the reeds.

"I *THOUGHT* WE MIGHT SPOT AN ALLI-GATOR HERE," Dad whispers. "LOOK AT HIM LURKING! HE'S WAITING FOR A BABY BIRD TO FALL OUT OF THE NEST! HE'S OUT OF LUCK, THOUGH. THESE BABIES ARE ALREADY BIG ENOUGH TO FLY ON THEIR OWN!"

It's almost sundown. The sky is slowly turning orange. You can see it reflected in the water.

The snowy egrets come gliding back to the branches of the trees.

They are pure white and their wings are almost three feet across. They have long, long necks and long, pointed beaks. And when they fly, their long legs stream out behind them.

Dad whispers, "WHAT A BEAUTIFUL SIGHT!"

"WOULD YOU BELIEVE," Dad continues, "THAT PEOPLE HUNTED THESE BIRDS UNTIL THERE WERE ALMOST NONE LEFT?! THEY USED THE FEATHERS TO DECORATE LADIES' HATS. THINK OF A WORLD WITHOUT SNOWY EGRETS! LUCKILY, WITH THE HELP OF SOME STRICT HUNTING RULES, THESE BIRDS HAVE COME BACK FROM THE EDGE OF EXTINCTION!"

Elton gets some good shots.

Then we drive on.

Janie sleeps the rest of the way, and I'm pretty tired myself.

It's dark when we get to the place where we're staying. It's called Cojo's Bayou Inn.

I stumble out of the car. Then I perk up. There's music playing! It kind of sways and bounces and makes you feel good.

A big man comes up to us. It's Cojo, the owner and cook of Cojo's Bayou Inn. He says, "Welcome to the bayou, land of magic and mystery!"

He pulls a quarter out of Jane's ear, and a baby crawfish out of mine! I'm sure that wasn't there before, because I would have felt it.

There is a big pot of spicy-smelling soup on the stove. Cojo says it's called gumbo, and he's been keeping it warm just for us. He ladles a thick and meaty spoonful over a bowl of rice. I didn't know I was so hungry.

Cojo winks at Jane and says, "You'll have sweet dreams tonight! The bayou, she will rock you to sleep."

I wonder what he means.

We walk to our cabin. The sounds of singing and laughter fade away, and you can hear the loud buzzing of insects.

Except guess what? Our cabin isn't a cabin at all — *it's a houseboat!*

CHAPTER THREE
COJO'S

I'm not planning on falling asleep right away — I want to check out the houseboat.

But it's dark, and I'm tired, and the next thing I know — it's morning!

I sit up in bed.

I hear a motorboat go by. *PUTTA PUTTA PUTTA PUTT PUTT.*

The houseboat bobs up and down in the wake of the boat. Is this cool or what?!

I jump out of bed.

I try to make the boat rock myself, but I guess I'm too light or something.

We have a bathroom with a toilet, and electric lights, and air-conditioning, and everything!

There's even a kitchen! It's just like a small house, but it's on the water! Awesome. I could *live* in a house like this.

I hear a thud. The houseboat dips and bobs. Then I hear my dad's big feet going *clomp, clomp*. He opens the door, sticks his head in, and says, "Are you guys up yet? Let's eat!"

I guess he got up early and went out exploring. I wish he had woken me up.

Mom calls out, "We'll be right there, Joe."

Even though we have a kitchen, we're going up to the main house to eat.

I go on deck with Dad.

We look over the side. The water is black and still. No, wait. I see some tiny ripples where it's flowing around a fallen branch.

A turtle plops off the branch into the water.

Dad says, "Spiny softshell turtle! Be careful handling those guys. They bite!"

He says, "This bayou is *teeming* with life! Listen."

I hear *brrapp, brrapp*. There are lots of frogs. Some of them go *peep, peep* and some of them go *gronk, gronk*. And there are birds chirping and singing. And insects buzzing. It's a pretty noisy place, actually.

But I don't see any alligators.

There's another boat next to our houseboat. Dad says that's the tour boat and we'll be going on it after breakfast. Cool!

Mom and Janie are ready.

The big trees along the banks are live oaks. That's their name. It doesn't mean they're alive. Even though they are.

Their branches are dripping with grayish plants that look like cobwebs. Those plants are called Spanish moss. Only they aren't really moss. I don't know if they're Spanish or not.

Dad says, "Spanish moss is an air plant. It gets all the water it needs straight from the air."

I reach up to touch it, but Dad puts his hand on my arm.

"That's not a good idea, son," he says. "There could be poisonous snakes in the tree branches. Snakes climb these trees sometimes, looking for birds' eggs. You wouldn't want one of them to fall on you!"

Then he pauses, and looks up into the Spanish moss. "You guys go on ahead," he says. "I'll catch up."

I look back and see him shaking one of the

branches. He'd love it if one of those poisonous snakes fell on *him*! Well, I guess that's why they call him Danger Joe.

"C'mon, Dad," I call. "Breakfast smells good!"

Elton and Lucy are already there.

Besides being the inn owner and the cook, Cojo will be our tour guide. Dad says nobody knows more about alligators than Cojo.

Minette is Cojo's grown-up daughter. She brings us our breakfast. Later on we meet Cojo's wife and his two grown-up sons and their wives and Minette's baby. Everybody helps out at Cojo's.

We have eggs with sweet potatoes and some little square muffins called *beignets*. Minette says that's how you spell it, but you pronounce it "bin-yay." It's French.

Minette says, "Beignets, they are like dough-nuts without the holes."

I ask Minette if Cojo comes from France.

She says, "Oh, no. Our ancestors, they came from France, way back. But my dad, he was born just south of here. On the coast. If he was born any closer to the ocean," she says, "he'd be a soft-shell crab right now!"

Jane looks at Cojo and laughs out loud.

Minette laughs, too, and gives Jane another beignet.

After breakfast, Cojo takes off his apron and puts on his hat.

He carries a little black box down to the tour boat.

"What's in there?" Janie asks him.

Cojo winks at her and pats the box. "This is my special alligator bait. We're going fishing for my friend Elvis. He is the World's Biggest Alligator!"

I can hardly wait to see the World's Biggest Alligator — and what Cojo has in the box.

CHAPTER FOUR
ON THE BAYOU

We board the tour boat and go chugging down the bayou, through the black water and beneath the Spanish moss.

An alligator slides off the bank and into the water. It disappears before I get a good look, but I'm sure it wasn't Elvis. It looked too small.

Cojo cuts the engine, and we wait and watch.

Then Cojo spots another alligator.

It's just lying there, half in, half out of the water. It looks like a bumpy old log.

Cojo says, "Alligator, he sets his own trap. Then Turtle, he comes along and thinks he sees a nice log. Turtle climbs up on the log, and he suns himself. Ol' Alligator, he don't move until

Turtle climbs off, then *chomp!* Quick as lightning, Alligator gets him."

Elton films the alligator, and Dad tells about it. Dad has this voice he uses on camera a lot. It's kind of a whisper, so it doesn't disturb the animals, but it's pretty loud.

"THIS IS THE AMERICAN ALLIGATOR!" he says. "WHAT AN AMAZING ANIMAL! IT'S THE BIGGEST REPTILE IN NORTH AMERICA!"

Dad says, "ALLIGATORS CAN WALK ON LAND. THEY CAN EVEN RUN AS FAST AS HUMANS FOR SHORT DISTANCES. BUT THEY ARE MOST AT HOME IN THE WATER, AND THEY'RE FAST SWIMMERS! THEY SWISH THAT BIG TAIL BACK AND FORTH" — Dad makes swishing movements with his arm to demonstrate — "AND THEY SHOOT THROUGH THE WATER! FASTER THAN A SMALL MOTORBOAT!"

The alligator doesn't move. He just lies there, looking like a log.

We turn off the main bayou into a smaller one. Elton has the camera ready.

Dad and Cojo are looking into the shallow water along the banks.

"Look there," says Cojo, pointing. "Swimming across."

I look, expecting to see another alligator. Instead I see — a rabbit!

I never saw a swimming rabbit before!

I hold my breath. I'm hoping a big ol' alligator won't rear up out of the muddy water and chomp down on that little rabbit!

Elton films Dad telling about the rabbit.

Dad says, "IT'S A SWAMP RABBIT! LOOK WHAT A GOOD SWIMMER SHE IS! AND SHE CAN DIVE, TOO. THERE ARE A LOT OF SWAMP RABBITS AROUND HERE, BUT WE'RE LUCKY TO SEE ONE. USUALLY THEY FEED AT NIGHT AND SLEEP UNDER A LOG DURING THE DAY. I GUESS SOMETHING SCARED HER. SEE HOW SHE'S HEADED STRAIGHT FOR THE OTHER BANK?"

We watch the rabbit until she reaches the other bank and disappears into the bushes.

Whew! I'm glad she made it!

The bayou twists and turns. We go off into a smaller stream.

We're just coasting now. Looking.

It's very still and dark under the trees.

This is a cypress swamp. The cypress trees have big roots that poke out of the water, and the roots have knobs on them.

Cojo says the knobs are called cypress knees.

He says, "But my Uncle Octave, he calls them witches' knees. Somewhere in this very swamp, he says, there's an old witch. She likes to sleep under the water with just her knees sticking up. Octave, he says if you bump the witch's knees, she will wake up."

The boat bumps gently into a cypress knee. Jane jumps and grabs on to Mom. Cojo gives her a big wink and a smile.

I think to myself, *If there are witches anywhere, this is the place they'd be!*

Cojo says, "Listen up, now!"

I listen to the swamp noises.

Then I hear a new sound — a kind of *chumpf, chumpf* noise.

31

"That's the sound of baby alligators coming out of their eggs!" says Cojo. He points out a big mound of grassy stuff.

We move the boat closer, and Elton starts the camera rolling.

Dad says to the camera, "THIS IS WHAT WE'VE BEEN LOOKING FOR! AN ALLIGA-TOR NEST!"

We approach the nest slowly.

Dad says, "THE MOTHER IS PROBABLY SOMEWHERE NEARBY. SHE USUALLY GUARDS THE NEST UNTIL THE EGGS HATCH. YEP! THERE SHE IS!"

We see her! At least we see her eyes and nose sticking out of the water. She's watching us, too.

Dad says, "AND THERE ARE THE BABIES! LOOK AT THAT!"

"Where?" says Jane.

Mom says, "Shhh." She points Jane in the right direction. Jane still has to learn not to talk while Dad's on camera.

There's one baby alligator in the water near the mother's head, and another one slithering down the side of the nest.

Dad says, "MANY REPTILES JUST BURY THEIR EGGS IN THE SAND AND LEAVE THEM THERE. BUT THE MOTHER ALLIGATOR BUILDS A BIG NEST HERSELF! SHE FINDS A NICE, HIDDEN SPOT — CLOSE TO THE WATER, BUT HIGH ENOUGH THAT IT WON'T GET FLOODED. AND SHE USES HER TAIL TO SCRAPE PLANTS AND MUD INTO A BIG PILE. THEN SHE PACKS EVERYTHING DOWN WITH HER BODY. FINALLY, SHE USES HER BACK FOOT TO SCOOP OUT A HOLE, AND SHE LAYS HER EGGS IN THE HOLE!

"WE'RE LUCKY TO FIND THESE BABIES RIGHT WHEN THEY'RE HATCHING OUT!"

We film the baby alligators for a long time. I count at least twenty of them. But Dad says there are probably more than that.

After a while there are no more *chumpf, chumpf* noises. The mother and her babies all slide under the water and disappear.

Cojo guides the boat up to the empty nest.

Dad gets out and pulls off some of the leaves and stuff, looking for the eggshells. He says, "DON'T TRY THIS IN YOUR BACKYARD! ALLIGATORS ARE PROTECTIVE OF THEIR BABIES. IN FACT, ANY ADULT ALLIGATOR THAT HEARS A BABY'S CALL FOR HELP WILL COME TO THE RESCUE. I THINK ALL OF THE EGGS HAVE HATCHED NOW, SO WE SHOULD BE OK."

He holds up an empty shell and says, "BABY ALLIGATORS HAVE A HARD, POINTED GROWTH ON THE ENDS OF THEIR SNOUTS. THEY USE IT TO SLICE OPEN

THEIR EGGS WHEN THEY'RE READY TO HATCH. IT'S CALLED A *CARUNCLE*."

He pulls aside more of the nest.

"THE MOTHER KNOWS WHAT SHE'S DOING WHEN SHE BUILDS A NEST," he says. "AS ALL OF THIS STUFF ROTS, IT PRODUCES HEAT AND KEEPS THE EGGS WARM."

Chumpf, chumpf.

What's that?

I think it must be Jane. She likes to imitate animal noises. I elbow her and say, "Shhhh."

"It wasn't me!" Jane says.

Chumpf, chumpf.

We all look at the nest.

Dad roots around in it, and finds one last baby, just coming out of its egg! He picks it up and holds it in his hand. Baby alligators are supposed to be about eight inches long, but I think this one looks even smaller than that.

Dad shows the baby alligator's caruncle to the camera, and Elton gets a close-up.

Jane says, "I WANT TO HOLD IT!"

Mom whispers, "Hush, Janie," but Janie has reached her limit for being good.

"I WANT IT!" she cries. "I want to take him home! Gumbo! I'm naming him Gumbo!"

Jane always wants to take animals home.

The baby alligator is going *chumpf, chumpf* for all he's worth.

Dad puts him down on the nest, and he heads for the water.

Jane is crying now.

Cojo says, "Gumbo, that's a good name for this little 'gator. But I'm thinking his mama, she will be looking for him."

The big alligator suddenly shoots out of the

water, right near the nest! There's a huge splash, and Dad leaps back into the boat.

Jane is so surprised, her crying turns into hiccups.

Gumbo slides down the side of the nest and lands on his mother's head. Jane laughs. We all laugh.

We watch him riding there as she swims away.

"You know what?" Cojo says to Jane. "Gumbo, he just might be the world's *smallest* alligator right now. I know *I* never saw a smaller one! But if you come back here in ten, twelve years, I'll show you Gumbo then. He'll be almost as big as Ol' Elvis, you bet!"

CHAPTER FIVE
OL' ELVIS

We go deeper into the swamp. We're looking for Ol' Elvis, the World's Biggest Alligator.

At least that's what Cojo calls him. But then Cojo winks and says, "You can believe me if you want to, because you know what? Some of what I say is true!"

I'm not sure I know what he means. Cojo also says, "The bayou, she is always changing. Sometimes she flows this way, sometimes she flows that way. Sometimes she is salty like the sea, sometimes she is not."

We turn a corner and the bayou opens up

into a small pond with grassy edges. You can see the sky again, and Cojo is looking at it.

"I don't like the look of that sky," he says. "After we see Ol' Elvis, we should head back, straight away."

We turn down a narrow, hidden stream. Grasses scrape the boat on both sides.

When the stream gets too narrow, Cojo pulls the boat into the mud and ties it to a tree.

We all get out of the boat. Cojo brings his black box, Elton brings his camera, and Lucy brings her notebook.

Elton steps onto a clump of grass that sloshes around like a bunch of wet noodles.

Cojo quickly pulls him to the next clump and says, "If you don't want to get wet, step where I step, like so."

Cojo points to one kind of grass. "See this grass?" he says. "She likes wet."

He shows us another kind of grass. "But this

grass," he says, "she likes dry. You want to step where the dry grass grows."

I look at the wet grass and the dry grass. I can't even tell the difference.

Cojo frowns at the gray sky. "Hurry along now," he says. "There's a big storm coming."

We hurry along, following Cojo from grass clump to grass clump. Some of them sink a little, and you have to jump, quick, to the next one.

A cold wind comes across the water.

We get to another, smaller pond. Cojo says it's a 'gator hole.

We stop and Elton gets ready to film.

Lucy says, "This is a beautiful location! It's so spooky! If we can get a good shot of Ol' Elvis, it will be great!"

Cojo says, "Ol' Elvis, he's like the bayou. He does whatever he wants to do. Sometimes he shows up, and sometimes he doesn't."

Cojo starts to open his black "alligator bait" box. I hold my breath. I try to guess what's inside. Raw chicken? I can't believe it when Cojo takes out, guess what — a fiddle!

He nods to Dad.

Dad says, "WE'VE COME TO THIS SPE-CIAL SPOT TO FILM WHAT MIGHT BE THE WORLD'S LARGEST ALLIGATOR! THIS 'GATOR HOLE BELONGS TO OL' ELVIS! OUR FRIEND COJO SAYS THAT OL' ELVIS MUST BE ABOUT FIFTY YEARS OLD. HE'S BLIND IN ONE EYE, AND HE'S MISSING SOME TEETH, BUT YOU STILL DON'T WANT TO MESS WITH OL' ELVIS!"

While Elton films the pond, or 'gator hole, Dad explains what it is.

"ALLIGATORS OFTEN MAKE THEIR OWN WATER HOLES. THEY USE THEIR TAILS AND MOUTHS TO PULL OUT GRASS AND DIG UP MUD, UNTIL THEY'VE MADE A NICE, BIG POND FOR THEMSELVES. WHEN THERE'S NOT ENOUGH RAIN AND IT GETS REALLY DRY, SOMETIMES THESE

'GATOR HOLES ARE THE ONLY AREAS OF WATER LEFT. THEY HELP MAINTAIN THE LIFE OF THE SWAMP!"

Everybody is listening to Dad and watching the 'gator hole. It seems as if even the frogs and insects are listening, because it's gotten very quiet in the swamp.

In his TV whisper, Dad says, "WE'RE GOING TO TRY TO GET THIS BIG 'GATOR TO COME TO THE SURFACE NOW. HE PROBABLY HAS AN UNDERWATER ESCAPE TUNNEL, SO WE DON'T WANT TO SCARE HIM OFF. BUT OUR FRIEND COJO IS A REAL LOUISIANA BAYOU GUIDE WHO KNOWS ELVIS LIKE AN OLD FRIEND, AND HE'S GOING TO TRY TO CALL HIM!"

Dad motions for the rest of us to move away from the hole.

Elton points the camera at the water.

Cojo draws his fiddle bow across the strings.

The fiddle makes an awful, low, sad wail.

45

Jane gasps and puts her hands over her ears.

Cojo does it again. The same long wail as before. *WOOOOAAOW.*

We wait.

Nothing happens.

Cojo looks up at the darkening sky and says, "Ol' Elvis, he knows a storm is on the way. Maybe he won't come out until it passes."

He takes off his hat and wipes his brow. "I think we should be getting back before the storm hits," he says. "We should give up now, and come back again tomorrow."

Lucy gives Dad a worried look. "What do you think, Joe?" she says. "We're on such a tight schedule." It's part of Lucy's job to worry about the schedule.

Of course, Dad *never* wants to give up. A little storm means nothing to him! He would stay out in a hurricane if he thought he could see the famous Ol' Elvis.

Mom and I know better, but we aren't in charge.

"Let's give it one more shot," Dad says.

Cojo grins and shrugs. "OK," he says. "We'll make it a good one!"

WOOOAAOWOW!

Jane isn't covering her ears anymore. In fact, I think she likes it. She's looking at Cojo as if she thinks he's a wizard or something.

And then, when nobody is really expecting it, we hear an answer that gives us goose bumps!

Almost like an echo, but deeper and louder, like a foghorn — it's an alligator bellow!

After the bellow, we hear a splash.

The surface of the water shimmies.

The cold wind moans.

A long, dark shadow passes underwater, right in front of us.

Then there comes the rumble of distant thunder. And then the water is all still again.

"Was that Ol' Elvis?" I ask in a whisper.

Cojo nods. "The thunder must have scared him off," he says.

We missed him.

BAM! There's a thunderclap. This time it's louder, and closer.

How did it get so dark so fast?

"We'd better leave now," says Mom. "I'm getting worried."

She looks at Cojo.

He says, "Mama is right. It's time to go."

He puts his fiddle back in its box. He looks at Dad with sad eyes, and shrugs. "What can I say? Another day, he will come."

Everyone is disappointed.

Elton lowers the camera and turns to go.

Then Jane opens her mouth. Did I mention Jane's big mouth? Sometimes what comes out of it surprises you.

She starts out low — "woooo." Then she gets louder and louder, "WOOOOAAAOWOW!" It's just like Cojo's fiddle!

I'm looking at Jane, and *my* mouth is hanging open. All our mouths are.

Then we hear that ol' 'gator bellow again. He's right behind us!

We whip around.

Elvis slaps his huge head against the pond, and all I can see is a spray of water.

I blink and wipe my eyes. Now I see him.

He almost fills the pond!

He swims in a circle, watching us.

You can see just how far it is from his head to the tip of his tail. And it's far! You can even see his pale, blind eye.

Dad yells, *"Galloping geckos! Get the shot! Get the shot!"*

Elton quickly lifts the camera.

There's a blinding flash of lightning and a huge, tooth-rattling **BOOM** of thunder!

And then the rain comes. And there's a burning smell in the air. And a tingling in my feet.

Dad says, "GOLLY! WHAT A WHOPPER! Elton, did you get that shot?!"

Elton doesn't answer.

CHAPTER SIX
SWAMP SEARCH

We all look at Elton.

The camera is in his hand, but it's hanging down by his side. He looks different. His hair is standing up, all around his head. There's a little cloud of smoke floating in the air above him.

He looks back at us and says, "Huh?"

Mom says, "Are you all right?"

Dad says, "Did you get the shot?"

Elton looks at the camera in his hand, and down at the pool of water. There's no alligator to be seen. Just drops of rain making circles in the water.

He shakes his head and says, "I don't know. I don't know."

We have to stand there in the rain for a while so Dad can ask Elton some questions. Like what's his name, and what year is it, and who's the president of the United States. Dad wants to make sure Elton still has all his marbles.

He seems to be all right.

Then Cojo takes us to a cabin in the swamp to wait out the storm.

When we get there, Elton checks the film.

Guess what?

He didn't get the shot.

The grown-ups don't think Elton got hit by lightning. They think he just felt the shock of it through the ground, like the rest of us.

But I am pretty sure he did. Nobody else's hair stuck out like that, smoking! And I know that another person got hit by lightning and lived. It was in the newspaper.

I keep looking at Elton. Hit by lightning! Now *that's* something you can tell your friends!

Elton might even develop some superpowers! Like ESP or something.

After the storm passes we have to hurry back to the inn, because Cojo has to make dinner for everyone staying there.

Dinner is fried crawfish, and shrimp and crabmeat *jambalaya*. That's one of Cojo's specialty dishes. You say it like this: "jum-buh-LIE-yuh." I'm not sure what it tastes like because it's too spicy-hot for me, and for Mom and Jane, too. Elton likes it, though. He eats a lot of it, and steam comes out his ears.

I wonder if that has anything to do with being hit by lightning.

Later I ask Elton what number I'm thinking of, because I want to see if he has ESP. (That stands for *extra-sensory perception*. It means you can see, or sense, things that normal people can't. It's like mind reading and stuff.)

Elton says, "Three hundred fifty-six."

I practically fall out of my chair! That's the number I was thinking of!

"What number am I thinking of now?" I say.

Elton looks at me and says, "Five."

Oh. Well, I was really thinking of ten. But I *did* think about five for a second.

And I think Elton probably *has* developed ESP from being struck by lightning, he just hasn't learned how to use it yet. I tell him that, and he just laughs.

The next morning, at breakfast, Cojo comes over to our table and sits down.

He says, "I went out again last night. Up to the 'gator hole. Ol' Elvis, he wasn't there."

Dad says, "Do you think he might be back this morning?"

Cojo shakes his head. "I dunno," he says. "I just dunno. Maybe that lightning did something to him. Maybe he's confused now and swimming far away, in a place he doesn't know. Maybe worse."

"What's worse?" says Jane.

Mom says, "Nothing, Jane. It's just an expression."

I know what Cojo means. He means Ol' Elvis might be dead! But I don't say anything.

Dad says, "Do you want to go out this morning and look for him? Lucy says we could put off the next part of our trip for half a day. We could do some more filming and keep our eyes open for Elvis. He might be nearby. Or on his way home. Alligators have a great homing sense, I know."

(Having a great homing sense means that they can find their way home from a long way off. Some other animals can do that, too. Like some dogs and cats. I read a book about it once.)

Dad adds, "And we'd love to have him on the show. I don't think there's another alligator that big anywhere!"

Cojo looks a little happier. "What did I tell you?" he says. "Ol' Elvis, he's the World's Biggest Alligator!"

We go out in the tour boat again. Mom brings an umbrella.

Cojo takes us down a lot of small bayous.

Sometimes he stops and makes his mournful call on the fiddle. We get Janie to do it a few times, too, but then she won't do it anymore.

Janie can be a pretty stubborn kid.

Ol' Elvis, he doesn't show up.

Elton whispers to me, "I don't think we'll find Elvis today."

"Why not?" I say.

"I dunno," says Elton. "It's just a feeling I have. I think he's far away from here."

I give Elton a long look.

"What other feelings have you got today?" I ask him casually.

Elton laughs. "Hunger!" he says.

We film some smaller alligators, but they aren't very exciting. Even Dad doesn't sound as enthusiastic as he usually does.

I don't think this will be a very good episode of *The Danger Joe Show* — not unless we can find Ol' Elvis!

We film a blue-tailed skink and a huge bull-frog.

Actually, I think the bullfrog is pretty cool.

Dad says, "THE AMERICAN BULLFROG IS NORTH AMERICA'S LARGEST FROG. AND THIS IS ONE OF THE BIGGEST I'VE EVER SEEN. HE MUST BE WELL OVER EIGHT INCHES LONG! MORE LIKE TEN OR TWELVE! AND HE'S A MIGHTY PREDA-TOR! DID YOU KNOW THAT A BIG BULL-FROG CAN CATCH AND EAT SMALL BIRDS AND SNAKES, AS WELL AS FISH AND INSECTS?!"

Dad says, "LET'S SEE IF I CAN CATCH HIM!" And he splashes into the water after the bullfrog.

We can hear the bullfrog in the swamp going

BARRRUMMM, BARRRRUMMM. But every time Dad gets close, he leaps farther away.

All this time, Cojo is looking for Ol' Elvis. He gets more and more sad-looking, as if Elvis were his lost pet. I guess that's how he feels.

We end up at the 'gator hole.

Cojo picks up his fiddle and makes it wail.

We all look deep into the water.

Nothing stirs at all.

"No way," says Elton, shaking his head. "He's not here."

I think, *Maybe Elton has developed a special bond with Elvis!* Because of the lightning. Maybe they both got struck at the same time, and electrical impulses jumped from one of them to the other! Sort of like the Incredible Hulk. Or Spider-Man.

"Are you still hungry?" I say to him.

"Yeah," he says. "I could go for some more of that jambalaya right now!"

I say, "What about raw fish?" and I watch him carefully.

He says, "Yeah, sushi would be cool!"

Aha! I thought so!

Later, when it's time to leave Cojo's Bayou Inn, Cojo says, "Some nights, you know, I'd go out to the 'gator hole and play my fiddle. And Ol' Elvis, he would sing along with me."

Mom wipes the corner of her eye.

Dad feels bad for making us stay and try to film Ol' Elvis in the storm. I know he does, because he told me so.

And besides, now we have to leave, and we didn't get a single shot of the World's Biggest Alligator.

Lucy gives Cojo a hug. She says, "I hope Elvis comes back."

Elton shakes his hand. "Thanks for the great food, Cojo," he says. "And don't worry about Elvis. I feel sure that he'll be back soon. He's just lying low for now. Maybe he didn't want to be on TV."

Cojo laughs and says, "Ol' Elvis, he's just another mean old alligator. The world, it can get along fine without him."

But I think that Cojo is just trying to act brave.

We wave and pull out of the driveway.

Dad says, "Who's watching out for car number two?"

I sigh. It's gonna be another long drive.

I start reading signs again.

"'REAL PIRATES!'" I read. "'HUNT FOR BURIED TREASURE!' Hey, Dad! That one sounds really cool!"

We drive on.

"'MERMAID LAGOON!'" I read on another sign. "'LIVE MERMAIDS IN A NATURAL SETTING! UNDERWATER VIEWS!'"

Dad drives on.

After we go a few miles, Jane says in an unusually serious voice, "I want to see the mermaids."

"We can't, honey," Mom says. "We're already late."

Jane says it louder. "I want to see the mermaids!"

"Now, Jane, sweetie, you've been so good all afternoon. I know it's a long drive . . ."

"I WANT TO SEE THE MERMAIDS!"

Uh-oh. This is it. A major meltdown.

Jane's wails fill the car. They practically break my eardrums.

Dad slows down. He pulls over.

Mom says to Dad. "She *has* been good all day, Joe. And we're all hot and tired."

Dad stops the car.

He takes Jane out of the car and walks her up and down the side of the road.

Elton and Lucy stop behind us, but they just wait in the car. They've seen this before.

When Jane stops sobbing, Dad puts her back in the car and gets back in the front seat.

"I told her," he says, "that we could stop somewhere tomorrow. It's too late now. But tomorrow, she can choose one roadside attraction, and we'll stop."

Jane says, "And Joey gets to choose one, too!"

You've got to love her for that! *Let's see,* I think. *What will I choose? I hope there's something good!*

Dad says, "That's right. Joe, Jr., can choose a stop for the following day."

Jane goes to sleep in her car seat. She looks exhausted and her cheeks are wet with tears, but there's a smile on her face.

CHAPTER SEVEN
MERMAID LAGOON

We spend the night in a motel.

The trouble starts in the morning. Jane wants to go back to Mermaid Lagoon.

Dad says, "We can't go back, Jane. We've got a long way to go today. When I said you could pick a spot, I meant a *new* spot, one that's on our way."

"You didn't say that," says Jane.

Dad says, "We don't have time to go back, honey. There will be good places coming up."

Jane folds her arms and says, "MERMAID LAGOON."

"But Janie," Dad says, "we've got to film the show! You know that."

"MERMAID LAGOON," she repeats. "That's what I choose."

Mom whispers something to Dad.

Dad talks with Lucy.

Lucy makes some phone calls.

"All right," Dad finally says. "We're going to 'MERMAID LAGOON.'"

Janie lets out a really loud alligator call, "WOOAWOO!"

"That will be enough of that, Miss Jane," says Mom.

We get in the car. Lucy and Elton get in car number two. (I have been watching Elton, by the way. He's been acting pretty normal so far, today.)

We head back the way we came yesterday.

I'm pretty interested to see these mermaids. I don't say so out loud, of course. I'm pretty sure there's no such thing as mermaids. But there *might* be. And remember, the sign said, "*LIVE* MERMAIDS."

From the outside, Mermaid Lagoon looks sort of like the aquarium we went to on our class trip.

Mom says, "Well, at least it's not just some two-bit backyard kiddie pool. This might be fun!"

Dad groans when he sees the prices. He takes out his wallet. "A kiddie pool might have been a little cheaper," he grumbles.

Mom laughs. "Oh, it's not that bad, Joe," she says. "Remember, this isn't just a working trip. It's our vacation, too."

Dad buys our tickets.

The girl at the ticket booth says that a show will be starting in five minutes, and that there's a gift shop to our left and a snack shop to our right.

Janie goes, "WOOOOAAWOW!"

The ticket girl looks startled.

Mom says, "All right, Jane. I don't want to hear that again. One more 'gator bellow out of you and we're leaving! Got that?"

She means it, too.

We go inside.

You go down a curved stairway and through a tunnel. Then you come out in an outdoor theater. Only it's half underground, with a big glass wall so you can see underwater.

It is so cool! There are plants and rocks and frogs and turtles and everything. It's just like you're in the bayou, except you can see underwater!

Mom is reading out of the brochure. "It says here," she says, "that this is a small natural lake with a bayou running through it. It has gates underwater at both ends. The gates let the water in but keep large aquatic animals out."

Aquatic means "living in water." I can guess what they mean by "large aquatic animals" — they mean alligators!

Mom continues, "The only way they've changed the lagoon is they cleaned up the muddy bottom and put in an island. And it says after the show you can go up and observe the life of the lagoon from a small stage."

There are stairs in the front of the theater. I guess that's the way to the stage.

Some music comes out of a loudspeaker.

The show is starting.

Two mermaids swim into view. And then two more. And two more. They do a sort of underwater dance.

You can tell that they're just pretty ladies who are wearing fishtail suits.

At least that's what I think.

They *do* look almost real.

I wonder.

Real ladies can't hold their breath that long, can they?

Maybe they've got gills, like fish! I try to see if they've got gills. I wish I had my binoculars.

Up above, a human man rows a boat to the

island. He's part of the show. He squats down and rinses his face in the water. He sees the mermaids!

The mermaids are afraid. They swim away and hide behind some rocks, but one of them peeks out.

My guess is that she's going to fall in love with the man. Like in *The Little Mermaid*.

I look at Jane. She's into it. Everything seems real to Jane.

I look back at the show.

Now a big alligator swims into the lagoon. *He* looks almost real, too.

The mermaids are terrified.

I laugh out loud. This is getting good!

The human man points at the alligator and yells to the audience. The mermaids are scrambling to get out of the water.

It seems so real that I'm sitting on the edge of my seat. Wow! I never thought Mermaid Lagoon would be this good!

One of the mermaids gets her tail caught on a rock. She looks frantic, trying to pull it free. She stares out at the audience through the glass. It looks like she says, "Help me!" Bubbles come out of her mouth.

The alligator swims in a circle and heads toward her. He's got a pale, blind eye, just like Ol' Elvis. That's funny. Why would you give a fake alligator a blind eye?

Suddenly, it occurs to me that this show is a little *too* real.

I jump up out of my seat. "Dad!" I yell. "Look! It's a *real* alligator! I think it's Ol' Elvis! They aren't acting anymore! *Do something!*"

Dad looks hard.

He says, "Good golly! I think you're right, son! How did he end up here?!"

He jumps out of his seat and runs up the front stairs, three at a time!

Next thing I know, he's diving right into the

lagoon with the alligator and the trapped mermaid!

"Dad," I say feebly. "I didn't mean you should jump in!" Of course, he can't hear me.

The mermaids are screaming.

The alligator is swimming in circles, looking at Dad and the mermaid with his good eye. I'm pretty sure it's Ol' Elvis. He must have broken through one of the underwater gates!

I don't like this, not one bit! But what can I do?

I get an idea.

"Jane!" I say. "Look! It's Ol' Elvis! Do you think you can call him with your alligator bellow and distract him, so he doesn't eat Dad and the mermaid?!"

Jane says, "Phooey! Daddy isn't afraid of that alligator."

Dad is trying to loosen the mermaid's tail. Mom is saying, "Oh, Joe! Oh, Joe!"

"I know," I say to Jane. "Dad isn't afraid of *anything*. But sometimes he can use a little help."

Jane gives me a look. "Just do it, Jane," I say. "It's important!"

She says, "Mom said that if I bellow again, we have to leave."

Now Dad is pushing against the rock, trying to move it. He can't move that big rock. Nobody could!

"No, Jane, this time it's OK," I insist. "It's an emergency. MOM! Tell Jane it's OK to bellow!"

Mom says, "What? Oh, good idea, Joe. Go ahead, Jane, quickly!"

But then the rock shifts! The mermaid pulls free. Dad saved her!

I relax. Except, uh-oh. To get out they have to swim past Ol' Elvis!

Dad's cheeks are all puffed out, and his eyes are bulging.

Jane looks at Mom. "You promise you won't make me leave?" she asks.

Aaaaargh! You can't hurry Jane, no matter how hard you try.

Mom says, "No, Janie honey. Do it now."

"All right." Jane takes a deep breath and goes, "WOOOOOOAWOOOWOW!" at the top of her lungs.

The alligator turns around.

Jane does it again.

The alligator swims to the surface.

Jane bellows a third time. (I think she likes doing it.)

The alligator bellows back. See? I knew it was Ol' Elvis!

Dad and the mermaid both shoot to the surface, then climb out of the water, gasping for breath.

There is a huge cheer from the audience.

Ol' Elvis bellows again and slaps his chin against the water.

CHAPTER EIGHT
'GATOR RESCUE

Now that I know Dad is safe, I go up and watch Ol' Elvis, the World's Biggest Alligator.

He's just swimming around.

I wonder what he's thinking. Dad is always teaching us to think like the animals. I'll try it out on Ol' Elvis.

Let's see. Ol' Elvis is probably thinking, *This lagoon is kind of boring after my nice 'gator hole. No mud, for one thing. And now the big guy and that lady with the fish tail are gone, too.*

Hey, I wonder if alligators know about mermaids?

Maybe Elton knows. He's the one who's supposed to have alligator ESP.

I look at Elton.

He's sitting there with a sort of grouchy look on his face. Maybe I won't ask him after all.

I don't know what he's got to be grouchy about. You'd think he would be *happy* that we found Ol' Elvis. And wait'll we tell Cojo! Think how happy he'll be!

I decide Elton probably doesn't have alligator ESP. He didn't even know Elvis would be here. *Janie* was the one who insisted on going to Mermaid Lagoon. And she can do the bellow, too. Hey, I wonder . . . !

I look at Jane. What if she . . . ?

Nah. I guess the whole ESP thing is just a silly idea. I *knew* it was, really.

Then Lucy says, "Elton, why don't you get the camera? This a good chance to get some shots of Ol' Elvis."

Elton doesn't even answer her. He's staring at Ol' Elvis with that same grouchy look. Now that I think about it, he's got kind of the same

expression on his face as Ol' Elvis! In fact, he's starting to *look* a little bit like Ol' Elvis! Hey, what if Elton is turning into *Alligator-Man*?!

Jane goes up to Elton and says, "Elton! Hey, Elton!" She shakes his arm.

"Hunh? Wha?" Elton gives her a startled look. Then he jumps up and says, "Right! The camera!" And he dashes off.

No, I guess he's not turning into Alligator-Man. Too bad.

I can see Dad and some man on the stage, looking over the lagoon. I think it's the manager.

The manager is yelling and waving his arms around. I guess he doesn't like having an alligator in his mermaid pool.

The ticket girl is there, too. She's leaning against the railing with her mouth hanging open, watching Ol' Elvis.

Now Dad is saying something to the manager.

I wish I could hear what's going on.

I see Lucy running up the stairs to join them, so I follow her.

Dad is saying, ". . . and they'll love it! Now, if you put a sign outside, 'WORLD'S BIGGEST ALLIGATOR — TODAY ONLY!' And get an announcement out on local radio. Think of the crowds you'll have!"

When Dad likes an idea, he can convince anybody.

"In fact," he says, "we'll feature 'Mermaid Lagoon' on our show. We'll get an alligator rescue crew in to capture Ol' Elvis and return him to his home. We can film it for *The Danger Joe Show*, and you can sell tickets! It will be great! Think of the free publicity! Mermaid Lagoon on national television!"

The manager is looking interested. I think he's gonna go for it.

Suddenly, it seems like everyone is rushing around making arrangements.

Mom takes Jane and me to have lunch in the snack shop.

Right after we get our food, Dad comes in.

He says, "Cojo's on his way! He's got a big boat to transport Elvis back up the bayou, and a team of alligator rescuers!"

He takes a bite of Mom's sandwich and rushes out again.

Now there's a line at the ticket window. The place is starting to fill up.

Mom and Jane go to claim our seats. I go to find Lucy and Elton.

Lucy has rewritten part of the show to include taking Elvis back to the 'gator hole.

Elton has already taken some shots of Elvis. I guess he doesn't want to miss his second chance at filming the World's Biggest Alligator. But hey, what could go wrong now?

I stand beside Elton and look over the railing.

I can't see Ol' Elvis, so I go down to where I can see underwater.

I still don't see him.

I ask a man in the front row where the alligator is.

He says, "The big 'gator? He just swam off to the left. Does that mean it's almost time for the show to start?"

I say I don't know, and I go looking for somebody who knows something.

The ticket girl is too busy selling tickets. Everybody is trying to get in to see the World's Biggest Alligator.

Except *where is he?*

Finally, I find Lucy. I tell her I can't see Ol' Elvis anywhere.

"What if he's gone?" I say.

Lucy gives me a horrified look. She gets Dad, and they look down into the lagoon.

"He can't be gone," Dad says. "They've got somebody guarding the broken underwater gate — that's how Elvis got in."

I say, "What about the other gate? If he broke one, why couldn't he break the other?"

Dad and Lucy look at each other. Then they rush off to check the other gate.

Dad comes back. "It's broken," he says.

Now we're really sunk. We've lost Ol' Elvis. Again!

"Don't worry," Dad says. "We'll find him."

He puts his hand on my shoulder. "Joe, Jr.," he says, "you watch for Cojo. Tell him what's happening, but don't tell anybody else! We don't want to start a riot!"

I wait for Cojo.

When he finally gets there, I give him the bad news.

"I was thinking," I say. "What if you played your fiddle? Maybe he would come then."

Cojo looks at me, thinking. "Might be worth a shot," he says.

"Yeah, and what about Jane? She could do her bellow, too."

"I'll see what your dad thinks. Which way to this broken gate?" Cojo asks.

I show him, and he and the rescue crew rush off.

Soon they are all back. Dad, too. "Where's Janie?" Dad says.

Everybody runs off in a different direction. Now they're all looking for Jane.

I say, "I know where she is." But everyone is already gone.

I go to tell Jane that everybody is looking for her. I'm wishing *I* was the one who could imitate an alligator's bellow.

Now the auditorium is full.

Nobody knows that Ol' Elvis is missing except us — the *Danger Joe* people and Cojo. Not even the manager knows.

He's not gonna like it.

Dad stands at the top of the steps with a microphone.

Elton is filming from the back row of seats.

Cojo and Jane are on the stage with Dad. Cojo is holding Jane's hand.

"You ready?" he says to her.

Jane nods.

Dad says, "HI, I'M DANGER JOE. SOME OF YOU WERE HERE A LITTLE WHILE AGO, WHEN OL' ELVIS, POSSIBLY THE WORLD'S BIGGEST ALLIGATOR, SURPRISED US BY COMING INTO THE LAGOON."

Some of the people in the audience hoot and wave their hands.

"WELL," says Dad, "HE JUST SURPRISED US AGAIN, BY LEAVING. BUT DON'T WORRY," he adds quickly. "I THINK WE CAN GET HIM TO COME BACK. ANYWAY, WE'RE GONNA TRY. AND IF WE CAN'T, WE'LL GIVE BACK YOUR MONEY!"

The manager jumps out of his seat. Lucy rushes over to talk to him.

Dad says, "HERE TO HELP US ARE COJO, THE ALLIGATOR EXPERT, AND YOUNG DANGER JANE, WHO IS AN ALLIGATOR CALLER! TAKE IT AWAY, COJO!"

Cojo draws the bow across the fiddle. **WOOOOOAAAOOW!**

Then Jane chimes in. **"WOWAAAOW!"**

The people in the audience are surprised. Some of them stand up so they can see better.

Then Elton does something funny. He hands the camera to Lucy and walks up the stairs to the stage. He's got that grouchy alligator look on his face again. What's the big idea?!

He says something to Dad.

Dad gapes at Elton for a minute, then he shrugs and laughs. "OK," he says. "FOLKS, WE'VE GOT ANOTHER ALLIGATOR EXPERT HERE. IT'S ELTON, THE ALLIGATOR PSYCHIC. ELTON TELLS ME OL' ELVIS IS

NEARBY, AND THE 'GATOR GAVE HIM A MESSAGE. ELVIS HEARS THE CALLS, AND HE HAS A REQUEST! HE WANTS COJO TO PLAY HIS FAVORITE SONG! IT GOES LIKE THIS . . ."

Dad holds the microphone up to Elton and Elton starts to sing into it! Holy cow! Elton would never do that if he was normal. He really *is* psychic!

Dad takes the microphone back. "THAT SONG SOUNDS LIKE *'LOUISIANA MAN'* TO ME. WHAT DO YOU SAY, COJO? DO YOU KNOW THAT TUNE?"

Cojo immediately starts playing the song, and Jane starts dancing. (What a show-off.)

The audience loves it. They're all standing up and clapping. Well, why not? I jump up and start dancing, too. It's a good song.

Elton whispers to Dad.

Dad says, "THE ALLIGATOR PSYCHIC SAYS ELVIS IS COMING!"

And guess what?! Here comes Ol' Elvis, swimming right in!

WOW! You should hear the crowd roar!

Ol' Elvis must like the cheering. Either that or he likes the song, because he stands up in the water and bellows.

Then Elton takes the microphone from Dad so he can tell us what Elvis is thinking.

Elton says, "Elvis tells me he doesn't like the look of those guys with ropes. He means the rescue team. He says he doesn't need to be rescued. Besides, he knows what rescuers do. They tie you up and put bags over your eyes and tell you it's for your own good. He says, 'Phooey.' And he'll bite anyone who tries it. He doesn't like it here, anyway. And he's leaving. He's going back to his 'gator hole. So get out of his way."

And Elvis charges out through the broken gate, swishing his big tail back and forth.

Elton looks kind of dazed and goes to sit down. I'm proud of him. Elton, the Alligator Psychic! I knew he got ESP when the lightning hit him! I knew it all along.

It's the best day ever at the Mermaid Lagoon.

We wrap up a great alligator episode of *The Danger Joe Show*.

And Cojo, he follows Ol' Elvis back up the bayou.

CHAPTER NINE
HAPPILY EVER AFTER

Back in our own house, I look at Jane.

Her face is resting on her toy koala. Her eyes are closed. Her breathing is slow and regular.

Good. She's asleep.

I get up. I don't make a sound.

I check to make sure Suni is asleep, too.

Then I tiptoe toward the door.

"Hey!" says Jane. "You didn't say, *And they all lived happily ever after*!"

Phooey! I thought she was asleep.

"Why aren't you asleep?" I say.

Jane looks at me like she can't believe how clueless I am. "Then I would miss the end of the story!" she says.

"But I can't leave until you're sleeping!" I say.

Jane smiles at me. "I know," she says.

I come back by the bed.

"So what does Dad usually do after he tells you a true adventure?" I ask her.

"He reads me *How Do Dinosaurs Say Good Night?*"

"Oh."

I pick up the book. I sit down. I read:

How does a dinosaur say good night

Jane snuggles down and closes her eyes.

When Papa comes in to turn off the light?

Jane starts breathing slower.

Does a dinosaur slam his tail and pout?

Jane starts snoring softly.

Does he throw his teddy bear all about?

I read the whole book. Just in case.

Besides, I like it.

Then I tiptoe out.

DANGER JOE'S CREATURE FEATURE
THE AMERICAN ALLIGATOR

John Shaw / Bruce Coleman Inc.

AMERICAN ALLIGATORS are large reptiles with big jaws and sharp teeth. Adult alligators usually grow to be six and a half to thirteen feet long, but people have reported seeing 'gators around eighteen feet long (and even longer!).

Alligators are closely related to crocodiles. They both belong to the animal group called *Crocodilia.*

All crocodilians share many of the same features. They have the most advanced brains of any reptiles. That means they can learn things and don't just act on instinct. They spend most of their time in or near water, and they eat both land and water animals.

Crocodilians have skin the color of mud, so they can hide on the floor of a water bed, waiting for food to come close enough. Then they launch a surprise attack! They do not chew their food. They can crush it and swallow it whole, or tear it and eat it in big chunks.

Crocodilians like to bask in the sun to get warm and then dive into the water to cool off. When they dive, they close up like submarines. Special valves close their ears and nostrils, and transparent eyelids protect their eyes.

They even have a special flap of skin that closes off their throats. That helps them to swallow food underwater without drowning.

Their heads are long and flat, with raised eyes and nostrils. That way, they can still see and breathe while the rest of their body is underwater.

They swim by swishing their big tails from side to side. As they glide through the water, protected by their thick waterproof skins, almost nothing can harm them.

Crocodilians are found in most parts of the world — wherever it is warm enough and wet enough, but American alligators live only in the southeastern United States.

Southern Florida is the only place that has both American alligators and American crocodiles. How can you tell them apart? The crocodiles have more pointed snouts, and their fourth, lower tooth sticks out over their top lip. It is also good to know that the crocodiles are fiercer and more dangerous than the alligators.

American alligators eat fish and frogs, swamp rabbits, turtles, rats, beavers, nutrias, raccoons, snakes, wading birds, minks, and otters. They are usually not a danger to human beings who take necessary precautions.

Crocodilians are amazing and important animals. They help control the life of our swamps and wetlands. And they have lived on Earth since the age of flying reptiles and huge dinosaurs!

DANGER JOE'S CREATURE FEATURE
THE SNOWY EGRET

M.H. Sharp / Photo Researchers

SNOWY EGRETS are beautiful white birds. They have long, thin legs for wading in the water of marshes and swamps, and long necks and bills for catching food. They eat water animals, like fish and insects and crawfish.

Adult snowy egrets are about twenty-four

inches long, and about forty inches from wing tip to wing tip. When they fly, they fold their necks into their shoulders and let their legs trail out behind them.

Snowy egrets are communal birds. That means they like to live and nest in groups. They often roost with other types of egrets — and with other kinds of wading birds, too.

During the mating season, snowy egrets grow long feathers to attract mates.

In the 1800s and early 1900s, feathers like these were often used to decorate women's hats. Millions of birds were hunted for their feathers. Especially snowy egrets! So many egrets were killed that they became a very rare and endangered species.

But laws were passed to save them, and fashions changed. Now, once again, the beautiful snowy egret can be seen throughout much of the United States.

DANGER JOE'S WILD WORDS

AMERICAN BULLFROG: The bullfrog is North America's largest frog. It is three and a half to eight inches long, yellow-green to brown in color, and has a loud, deep croak.

BALD EAGLE: Bald eagles are large, soaring, meat-eating birds. They have white heads and tails, and brown bodies. They measure about eighty inches from wing tip to wing tip.

BAYOU: A bayou is a watercourse or slow-moving stream. The word comes from a Choctaw Indian word for creek — *bayuk*.

BLUE-TAILED SKINK: Skinks are a type of smooth-skinned lizard. There are three kinds of blue-tailed skinks common to the south-eastern United States.

CARUNCLE: A caruncle is a growth. Baby alligators, in the egg, can slit their shells open with the hard, pointed caruncle on their snouts.

CRAWFISH: Crawfish are not fish. They are water creatures that look like small lobsters. In many places they are called *crayfish*, but in Louisiana they're known as *crawfish*.

CYPRESS: The cypress trees that are common to Louisiana swamps are called *bald cypress*. They grow in swamps because their young seedlings need constant moisture, and because there isn't much competition for sunlight from other, taller trees, most of which don't like having their roots flooded.

EXTINCTION: When something becomes extinct, it no longer exists. The word *extinction* is often used when a whole kind of animal is wiped out. Many types of plants and animals that used to live on this planet have become extinct — like dinosaurs, for example.

GILLS: Gills are parts of the bodies of fish and other animals that live underwater.

These animals use their gills to get oxygen out of water, and that's how they breathe.

LAGOON: A lagoon is a shallow body of water.

LIVE OAK: Live oaks got the name "live" because they are evergreen. They do not appear dead and leafless in winter like many other trees. They grow in the South, and are valued for their beauty and for the cooling shade their widely spreading branches provide.

MARSH: A marsh is a place where the ground is soft and wet. It is mostly treeless, with tall grasses and cattails growing in the soggy ground. Marshes are often located between bodies of water and land.

MERMAID: Mermaids are imaginary women of the sea. They have fishlike tails instead of legs.

SPANISH MOSS: Spanish moss is a grayish air plant that hangs from the branches of southern trees and lives on air, rain, dust, and dew.

SPINY SOFTSHELL TURTLE: This turtle has webbed feet, a long, flexible neck, and a flat, hard shell that is covered with a soft skin. It can grow to about twenty inches long, and it catches and eats crawfish and small fish. It is known for having a vicious temper and will bite if disturbed.

SWAMP RABBIT: Rabbits are small- to medium-sized, plant-eating animals. Swamp rabbits look like common cottontail rabbits, but they are larger (up to twenty-two inches long), and they swim and dive with ease. They live in marshes and swamps and eat grasses and water plants.

ABOUT THE AUTHORS AND ILLUSTRATORS

Creating *The Danger Joe Show* books takes a lot of teamwork. Jon Buller does more of the illustrating, and Susan Schade does more of the writing, but they both do some of each. In addition to their Danger Joe titles, they have published more than forty books, including *20,000 Baseball Cards Under the Sea* and *Space Dog Jack*. They are married and live in Lyme, Connecticut, where they can often be found walking in the local forests, looking for mushrooms, and paddling kayaks in local rivers and streams. They used to have two pet snails, but they decided to release them back into their natural habitat.

THE DANGER JOE SHOW

TAKE PART IN ALL OF
DANGER JOE'S ANIMAL ADVENTURES!

Growling Grizzly

Bungee Baboon Rescue

Hawk Talk

Back to the Bayou